Day 1

I have not been in such an unusual situation since I once fell into a cesspit whilst escaping an angry deer[1]. (Accidentally, of course, as if anyone would do such a thing on purpose.) I am now officially a spy and have been instructed to keep a diary, should England's spymaster, Lord Severn, require information from me at a later date.

---

1   There were plenty of deer around in Tudor England, and large male deer with big antlers could kill a person. And people drowned in cesspits too!

My uncle, Lord Snoop, an advisor to the young king[2], hath been a friend of Lord Severn for many moons, though they are rarely seen together, and it is he who suggested Lord Severn approach me for this task. I am honoured that my uncle thinks me worthy and that Lord Severn agrees! My sister, Beth, sees me as bobolyn![3]

My quill skills[4] are far from perfect, and my fingers are already

---

2   King Edward VI, son of Henry VIII, came to the throne aged nine. He had two much older half-sisters – each was born to a different mother – but he became monarch because he was male.

3   A splendid Tudor word for an idiot!

4   Quills were pens made from feathers – with a nib cut into one end – and dipped in ink.

To the staff and volunteers who have made
my visits to National Trust properties, over
fifty years, fun and informative.

PA

First published in the UK in 2018 by Nosy Crow Ltd
The Crow's Nest, Baden Place, Crosby Row
London, SE1 1YW, UK

The words 'The National Trust' and the oak leaf logo are registered trademarks of the
National Trust for England, Wales and Northern Ireland used under licence from
National Trust (Enterprises) Limited (Registered Company Number 01083105).

Nosy Crow and associated logos are trademarks and/or
registered trademarks of Nosy Crow Ltd

Text copyright © Philip Ardagh, 2018
Illustrations © Jamie Littler, 2018

The right of Philip Ardagh and Jamie Littler to be identified as the author
and illustrator respectively of this work has been asserted by them in accordance
with the Copyright, Designs and Patents Act 1988.

A CIP catalogue record for this book will be available from the British Library

Printed and bound in the UK by Clays Ltd, St Ives Plc

Papers used by Nosy Crow are made from wood grown in sustainable forests.

ISBN: 978 1 78800 055 0

www.nosycrow.com

as black as an inky crow[5], so I do expect the occasional blot, blob and splatter to accompany my all-important words. Not only that, I must write everything in this special code[6].

The code was provided to me by none other than Lord Severn himself, in case this record of events should fall into enemy hands.

If it were to do so, my writings would make about as much sense as a man bridging a river without a pole.[7]

It is honour enough to be working as one of the king's youngest spies – I am aged just three years and ten[8] – but to be trained by Lord Severn in person is beyond my wildest of dreams (and my dreams have been mighty wild upon occasion, such as the one I had about the tiny blacksmith and the giant

---

5 No, we don't know what he was on about either.
6 Fortunately, it has recently been decoded, which is why the language is not QUITE as actual Tudor English would have been written or spoken. In fact much of it is FAR more modern… but easier to read!
7 Many smaller rivers and streams out in the countryside had no bridges built across them. Locals would pole-vault across them instead!
8 3+10 = 13, so he's twelve-and-a bit.

pelican[9]). I have much to be thankful for.

Though I have yet to receive my final instructions, I have been ordered to start this diary today so that I might practise writing in this confounded code. I confess that I have not yet fully mastered it, so suspect that I shall make the occasional *[cake]*[10].

My name is Thomas Snoop and I have been tasked in helping the fight against fellow Englishmen who are plotting, hand in glove, with a foreign power: The Spanish! Shocking I know, but true! (Gloves are optional.)

I am a good true Protestant[11] which meaneth that my greatest enemies are the followers of Rome[12], whether they be at home or abroad. There are Catholics in this country who hide their true faith and pretend allegiance to our protestant King Edward and the

---

9   In Tudor times, the pelican represented self-sacrifice and a charitable nature.

10   I suspect the word he intended to write here – in code, remember – was not 'cake' but 'mistake'... but he made one.* (*A mistake that is, not a cake and, anyway 'cake' meant 'loaf' in Tudor times.)

11   A Christian who does not follow the Roman Catholic faith.

12   Not a football club, or even the Romans in the Julius Caesar sense of the word, but the Roman Catholic Church with the Pope at its head. (Protestants are non-Catholic Christians.)

Anglican Church[13]. For them I may have some sympathy, though I voice it not aloud[14], for – once upon a time – we Christians were all Catholic also.

The real danger lies in those Catholics not content in simply carrying on the religion behind closed doors, but in plotting with foreign allies, such as those from Spain. Their shocking aim? To have a Catholic King back upon the throne of England! What TRAITORS!

13   The Anglican Church is the Church of England, founded by Henry VIII.
14   And probably shouldn't have mentioned in his diary, either!

Not a day doth pass without rumours or intelligence[15] about certain seemingly respectable *[hobble hen]*[16] holding secret talks with envoys from Spain. Lord Severn hath received information that two such traitors will be amongst the many noblemen and noblewomen soon to be residing as guests of William de Grieff[17], Earl of Drayshire, at his most beautiful manor house, Goldenhilt Hall. My mission is to find out who they are and what evil plans they have afoot! (Feet optional.)

---

15 The collection of information of military or political importance by spies, etc.
16 By 'hobble hen', I suspect he meant to say 'noblemen'.
17 Noble English families often had French-sounding names because William the Conqueror – who became King of England back in 1066 – was from French-speaking Normandy and gave English lands and titles to his Norman knights.

Even the name Goldenhilt soundeth beautiful, *hilt* being the name for a handle of a sword and *golden* being all – well – golden, as in gold! (And who doth not like a bit of gold?) 'Tis said to be one of the most spectacular houses in all England!

Lord Severn hath somehow arranged for me to be assigned the position of assistant to Master Tundy, the steward[18], who is charged with running all aspects of the Goldenhilt Hall household. As far as I am aware, no member of the household knows the true purpose of my employ[19].

Even Master[20] Tundy believes that I will simply

---

18 The Steward of the Household was the most important servant in a grand Tudor house. He – always a he, like most servants – was in charge of all the servants and carried out his master and mistress's wishes.

19 In other words, no one there will know what he's really up to.

20 A term for 'Mister'. A sign of respect.

be arriving to assist with the arrival of noble personages. He is most obviously a man used to being privy to most of what happens under Goldenhilt Hall's roof (which, I am informed, is beautifully decorated).

I am currently residing in the home of Lady Margaret P—, a close confidant to Lord Severn, which I suppose maketh her a form of spy also. I am to begin my journey to the Hall on the *[marrow]*[21]. I call her Lady Margaret P— not to hide her true identity but because I find her name ~~unspelible unspelable unsp~~ impossible to spell! I think it rhymes with kirtle.[22]

<hr />

21   I think he meant 'on the morrow' which simply means 'tomorrow', rather than 'marrow' which is a vegetable a bit like a VERY fat cucumber.
22   Rather confusingly, a kirtle was either a woman's gown or a man's cloak.

Day 2

This morning, Lady Margaret P— (whose name I cannot spell, but which rhymes with myrtle[23]) – summoned me to her chamber and dismissed her ladies in waiting, who surround her like a pack of hunting dogs surroundeth the master of the hounds[24]. Some are pretty and some more like horses[25], but all smell of sweet herbs[26] and of powders. Lady Margaret smiled as they left. The minute the great door was closed behind them, however, her expression changed to that of a stern preacher who hath not heard a good joke in a long while, or hath fallen victim to a bad smell.

"You are ready, Thomas?" she enquired, leaning forward in her fine chair, the only one

---

23   A type of shrub/bushy plant.
24   Hunting with hounds was a very popular pastime for wealthy Tudors.
25   Henry VIII, a Tudor king, described his fourth wife, Anne of Cleves, as 'the Flanders Mare'; Flanders being a country and 'mare' being a female horse. This unkind comment was made because she'd looked beautiful in her portrait, and it was on that basis that he'd agreed to marry her, their never having met.
26   People rarely washed and the rich disguised their body odour in many ways. Dried lavender was a popular choice.

in the room[27]. "The guests begin to arrive at Goldenhilt Hall over the next few days, and you must be our eyes and ears." She hath nice ears. And her two eyes be nice also.

---

27 People usually sat on stools or even cushions on the floor. Chairs were for important people: a sign of status.

"I AM READY AS I'LL EVER BE, MY LADY,"

I said with much honesty.

She nodded. "Good," she said. "You know the code?"

"I have almost mastered it, mistress," I assured her. "I'm a fast *[burner]*[28]."

"That is good," she said. "Lord Severn hath trained you well. Now find you my man Rowan and make haste to the Hall," she instructed. "He hath with him all the provisions you will need."

"Yes, mistress," said I, and made to walk towards the door. Rowan is her trusted servant, but even he does not know of my spying or my mission.

"Wait!" she instructed. "Take this." From her flowing sleeve she produced a pendant strung on a piece of leather to place around my neck. I studied it. It was carved of bone in the shape of a rabbit poking its head out of a gap

---

28   He must, surely, have meant 'learner'?

between parted grass. It had a toothy smile that reminded me of my father's servant, Hogg. "For luck," she explained.

"Thank you, my lady!" I said, accepting the talisman.

"God's speed!" she replied.

I found Rowan preparing two horses in the stables. He is a stocky Welshman of some eight-and-twenty years, with dark hair and eyes as black as night (on a particularly black night). You could not find a man more loyal to our noble Tudor king.

With provisions slung in saddle-bags across our two horses, we set forth for Goldenhilt Hall, watched only by the Yeoman of the Horse.[29] Who knows what *[trenchers]*[30] lie ahead?

---

29   In charge of the stables.
30   Adventures? Challenges? Or maybe he did mean trenchers after all!

Day 3

After a day's uneventful riding, in which
little occurred beyond my acquiring a tender
behind[31], we spent our first night in a tavern
situated near one of the King's Posts.[32] Two
of the posts' men responsible for delivering
communications had already had too much
to drink when we arrived. They were laughing
and joking. By the time we had each been
served and eaten a most acceptable umble

31 A sore bum.
32 This was a part of remarkable network set up by Henry VIII
    whereby letters could be delivered across the country by horse,
    stopping to collect and deliver mail at various posting stations,
    where the riders could also stop and rest. This is why letters and
    parcels are still referred to as 'post' today, why we have a 'postal
    service', 'post offices' and 'postmen' and 'postwomen'. All because of
    these Tudor posting stops along the original routes.

pie[33], they were barely able to sit without slumping their heads upon the table, where sat their discarded meal and yet another flagon of ale. One had his head in a plate of gravy. Neither he nor the gravy seemed to mind much.

33   Umbles were the heart, liver kidney and lungs of an animal, so that's what an umble pie contained. Today, these are often thought of as the cheaper, less-nice bits of meat – and is where the phrase 'eating humble pie' comes from, meaning being submissive – but tastes change. In Tudor times, the umbles were often seen as the *best* bits!

I suspect that they – the two men, not the one man and his gravy – might be somewhat delayed on the morrow, and that the letters may take a little longer to be delivered!

Rowan and I shared a bed and his snoring kept me awake much of the night, which is odd for he complained that my snoring had kept *him* awake, so *one* of us must have been lying.[34] After a breakfast of bread and ale,[35] we began our journey once more.

Much of the morning's riding took us through forest[36] where a tree root was to be my downfall. Literally.

My horse, a mare by the name of Nimblefoot (Ho! Ho!), caught one of her hooves in a root jutting out from the mossy ground and, as she lurched forward, I took the plunge.

---

34   It was common for people to share beds when travelling.
35   Water was often unclean and tasted unpleasant, so ale was a better choice.
36   Much of England was still covered in woodland at this time.

My pride was hurt at least as much as my bottom.

"Are you unharmed, Master Thomas?" asked Rowan, sliding from his horse in one easy movement and helping me to my feet.

I rubbed my bottom. "I'll live," I said and smiled sheepishly.

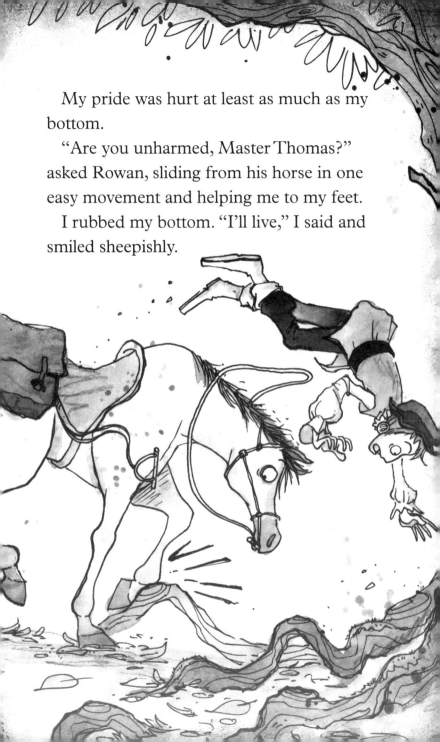

At that moment, a man appeared between the trees. He was the size of a small village and about as wide. I exaggerate of course, but to say that he was a mountain of a man would not do his physique justice. He was the biggest human being I have ever seen and ever expect to see. I did not dream that such LARGENESS could exist in human form! If I were to see him often, I might require bigger eyes.

"And what have we here?" he said, his voice as deep as a well and loud enough to startle a flock of birds from the trees. How do I know? Because, when he spoke, he startled a flock of birds from the trees. (See? My recording of events is most methodical.)

I pulled myself to my fullest height, which did little more than further emphasise the difference in size between us, like an ant standing upon tip-toe next to a carthorse, or a wren trying to impress a falcon[37]!

---

37   Falconry – the hunting of smaller birds with birds of prey – was a popular pastime amongst nobility in Tudor times.

"We are mere travellers passing through," said Rowan, "and who, pray, are you?" Rowan sounded both calm and relaxed, as though he talked to giants in forests every day but weekends.

The mighty man laughed. "Were you not warned that it is best to remain on the more oft-ridden roads?" he said. "Who knows what dangers lie within?"

"I have ridden this path many times," said Rowan, "and am well aware of the dangers and where best to tread." This might have sounded more impressive had Rowan's treading not just resulted in his stepping in some boar's[38] dung, which he was now busy trying to wipe off on a tufty tuft of grass.

The man came a step closer, casting a huge shadow over the pair of us. I saw now what he was holding in his hands. I had, at first, mistaken it for a furry coat or blanket or sack, or even a spare beard. I could see now that it was a dead wolf[39]. He threw it upon the ground before us.

---

38   Wild boar – a kind of tusked pig – lived in many British forests. They were hunted for sport and boar's heads were a specialty dish in nobles' houses.

39   Wolves were also common in England at the time. The last wolves died out in around the seventeeth century.

"It is fortunate for the pair of you that I walked this path before you," the stranger continued, "for I do not imagine either of you has the strength to kill such a beast with your bare hands."

"Most fortunate," said Rowan, sounding unconvinced. "Might we know your name?"

The ogre looked at us with his slate-grey eyes. "My name is Green," he said.

I thought of the Wild Man of the Woods carved into the woodwork of our churches[40], nestling amongst the saints and holy people,

---

40   Today, such carvings in churches are referred to as The Green Man, and he is seen as a symbol of fertility and growth.

bearded and surrounded in foliage: a pagan symbol predating Christ's words in this land.[41]

And I thought of the men dressed in leaves and green who head up processions in the towns and villages, wielding big sticks and throwing firecrackers to attract attention and clear the way. But these are merely men in costume, whereas Green did look very much like the real article!

"I am Rowan," said Rowan. Well, he would would he not? "Named after Mountain Ash."[42] Rowan put his hand in his pocket and produced a sprig cut from a branch. "'Tis a fine protector against witchcraft and the like.[43]" He looked hard at the giant as though he were just the kind of magical being from whom we needed *[nosebags]*[44]. "But we must be on our

---

41 Christianity was first brought to Britain by the Celts in around AD37. It was later spread by the Romans in the third and fourth century. The man later known as St Augustine was sent over to England by the Pope in 595 and became the first Archbishop of Canterbury in 597.
42 Mountain Ash is a popular folk name for the Rowan tree.
43 Tree lore – the folklore of trees – attributed different powers and attributes to different types of tree.
44 The word should probably be 'saving'.

way again," he said. "Good day to you."

The giant of a man nodded.

I had decided by now that if this man were planning to rob and kill us or even kill and rob us – whichever he found the easier and most convenient – he would have done so by now.

I had not spoken throughout our brief encounter – no one can accuse me of being a jangler![45] – but I gave a nod in return before turning to Nimblefoot. I slightly lost my dignity when attempting to remount her. She must still have been skittish from becoming entangled in the tree root and decided to step forward just as I was swinging my leg over her. I am still unclear as to how I found myself to be facing the wrong way. For a moment, I was puzzled as to what had happened to her neck and head…

… until I realised that they were behind me!

---

45   Chatter-box.

Once both Rowan and I were aback our mounts, and facing in the right direction, we bade the giant Green farewell and resumed our journey to Goldenhilt Hall.

The rest of the day was without event.

Day 4

I cannot state how eager I am to reach Goldenhilt Hall, not just in excitement of my actual mission but because of reports of the house itself. It is said to be one of the very finest in all England, with much of it built in the very latest style, with grand windows and doorways and high chimneys. Small wonder that many people of the greatest *[poor ants]*[46] have accepted the Earl of Drayshire's invitation to stay there.

I was pondering all this last night, whilst studying a rough layout of the gardens[47], at a table in another tavern, even less reputable than the last. The mistress – a boss[48] – who served us wine and ale looked as though she could wrestle a bear[49] and win. She turned a

---

46 I think he must have meant 'importance'.
47 Formal Tudor gardens were a maze of beautiful patterns and designs of plants and shrubs and hedges, often including an actual maze.
48 Not a boss as in 'someone in charge', but Tudor slang for a large woman.
49 There were no wild bears left in England by Tudor times, but there were captive bears used for 'entertainment'.

man from his lodgings so that we might have a bed for the night.[50]

We stumbled upon the poor man the next morning when claiming our horses[51]. He was fully clothed, lying face-down in the stable. He was either inspecting something on the ground very close-to, or was still sleeping where she had dropped him.

---

50   With the existing occupant drunk, and Snoop and Rowan obviously wealthier, the chance to make more money by giving them the room would not have been uncommon in less reputable establishments!

51   In 1557, a visitor to England from continental Europe was surprised by just how many people road horses. Not just the rich and nobles, as was often the case in other countries, but also, he commented "there is no male or female peasant who does not ride on horseback." More people were injured by horse than any other animal, wild or domestic!

The day's riding was uneventful. At one stage we passed the home of my late uncle, Lord Alfred Carp, my mother's elder brother. Having no son and heir, his lands and title passed to a cousin, Geoffrey, who will, in turn, pass it on to his son.[52]

"It was Uncle Alfred who taught me our island's history, when I was a boy of eight," I told Rowan.

"And did he tell you that our great English kings are from Welsh stock?" he inquired, raising an eyebrow and a smile.

I do, indeed, know our country has been ruled by members of the Tudor family since Henry Tudor[53] won the throne from bad King Richard.[54] And I do know that Henry had

---

52 This was common practice. The oldest male child inherits the nobleman's title. If there is no son, the title moves sideways to the oldest remaining brother, or failing that, a nephew or even cousin. With royalty, it was slightly different. If there was no son to inherit the crown, it could pass to the oldest daughter. As in the case of King Edward VI, the son could be younger than all his sisters, though, and still be the first in line to inherit. This has now changed with the UK monarchy. Now the oldest child of any king or queen will inherit the crown, regardless of whether they are male or female.
53 Who became King Henry VII.
54 Richard III. Snoop would say that Richard was bad, of course, because those who win wars can rewrite history.

ruled the principality of Wales[55].

It is evening now and we have pitched tent. I am writing by firelight. All being well, tomorrow we should reach the Hall.

55 The royal household had divided into two warring factions, the Yorks and the Lancastrians, each fighting for the crown under the emblem of their rose; the Yorks' rose being white and the Lancastrians' red. Henry Tudor was a Lancastrian but, on becoming King Henry VII, married Elizabeth of York, thus uniting the two houses and forming a new rose, of both white and red: the Tudor Rose.

Day 5

This evening, we finally
reached Goldenhilt Hall
at dusk without
incident. As
we rode up the
sweeping driveway,

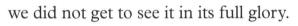

we did not get to see it in its full glory.
I look forward to the morning, and am too
tired to write anymore now. My bed is calling
me like a rock might call a crow to perch upon
it, if rocks could talk and liked crows sitting on
them. See? I am so tired I am making little, if
any, sense![56]

---

56   This paragraph was PARTICULARLY difficult to decode!

Day 6

Upon our arrival last night, Rowan and I stabled our horses ourselves and I was shown to my chamber by a kitchen lad named Peter. (He is small and grubby with big eyes and the smile of a naughty imp. I like him!)

Despite rising at an early hour, Goldenhilt Hall was already teeming with people. With so many guests of great import arriving at the Hall this week, many have sent their representatives and servants ahead of them to ensure that all is to their satisfaction upon their arrival. The most important guests expect the best rooms.

The hall is every bit as glorious as I imagined! More so, even. It has a forest of chimneys of every shape and design, patterned in brick. Every archway and every window, every flagstone and downpipe has been perfectly proportioned with an artist's eye. It cries out modernity and sophistication![57]

"The problem," said Master Tundy, the steward, when I was taken to meet him this morning after breakfast, "is that how important a person *considers* himself to be in the order of things and how important *others* may consider him to be can be two separate matters all together!"[58]

Master Tundy was sitting behind his enormous desk in his office. He is a large man; not particularly in height but in girth. He hath no gorebelly[59] but is, rather, round like a ball! In sooth,[60] he is about as round a man as I

---

57   Thomas may be getting a bit carried away here, but he's right in that such houses were built by the very wealthy as status symbols to show of just how rich they were and how many guests they could house and servants they needed. They could also show off how fashionable and up-to-the-minute they were with the latest architectural fads.

58   There was a very particular hierarchy – order of importance – in English aristocracy in Tudor England.

59   Paunch.

60   Truth.

could ever expect to meet, but he is imposing with it. He hath a kindly face with neat-trimmed beard, but also the manners of a man used to being obeyed and taking NO nonsense.

"How do you mean, sire?" I asked.

"Without a doubt, the Most Noble[61]

---

61   Master Tundy isn't just being respectful – a duke really is titled 'the Most Noble'!

Thomas[62] Casement, Duke of Hampton, is the highest ranking guest and will be afforded the finest quarters,[63]" the steward explained, "and no one would contest that, but *after* his grace, there are many who feel that they should be awarded the next-best quarters!" He then proceeded to give me instructions to pass on to others regarding the airing of the bedrooms in the less-often-used east wing.

"Yes, sire," I nodded.

After issuing many an instruction on Master Tundy's behalf and reporting back to him whether things had or had not been done at his insistence, I caught sight of a familiar face in a basement corridor.

It belongeth to Mark Tollman, a friend who used to live upon an estate bordering my uncle's lands, whom I have known since birth. He is here, it transpires, as the advance party to his master, one Lord Mulberry. He was surprised to find me working here at

---

62   Thomas was a very popular name in Tudor England amongst very powerful men.
63   Best bedroom/nicest suite!

Goldenhilt Hall. I was surprised to see that he had a swollen face and a black eye.

"Were you attacked on your way here?" I asked with much concern. "Are there robbers abroad?"[64]

---

64   Not 'abroad' as in a foreign country. It simply means out and about.

He shook his battered head and told me an extraordinary tale, which I went away and committed to paper from memory, in note form, as soon as I was able. I will now retell it here:

BEING AN ACCOUNT BY MARK TOLLMAN
OF HIS JOURNEY TO GOLDENHILT HALL,
TOLD TO ME, THOMAS SNOOP, IN AS MANY
OF HIS OWN WORDS AS I CAN RECALL

On our second day of riding, John Rider and I drew near the village of Hamble Hooe. I was surprised by how few other people there were about the place. The windmill stood idle[65] and there was a sign of neither the miller nor his apprentices.[66] The village square was clear of any market stalls.

John and I dismounted and he led the horses to a trough of rainwater from which they began to drink.

It was then we heard a distant roar. I have never heard anything like it, Thomas. What could it be? A rumble of thunder? A giant wave dragging a thousand pebbles in its undertow? For one fleeting moment, I even considered the

---

65   The Tudors used both wind and water power – windmills and watermills – to operate machinery to turn huge mill stones, between which grain was ground into flour.

66   A person would learn a trade by being apprenticed to his master. In this case, the miller would feed and house the boy, who would work without pay but learn a trade in return.

possibility of it being the roar of a dragon, that beast of folklore and of heraldry[67].

A moment later, the horses bolted; galloping off the way we came, nostrils flared and eyes wide with fear.

And then they appeared. Hundreds of them. Shouting, charging, jeering, cheering, running, falling, tripping, hobbling, squalling, calling, frightening, appalling people.

One of them threw something in our direction and instinctively, thus without a moment's contemplation, I ran forward and caught it.

If only I had let it lie, things might have taken a very different turn.

As it was, I looked down in horror as realisation dawned. I had in my hands a pig's bladder stuffed with beans and peas.

A moment later, the mob was upon me.

We had found ourselves in the middle of a game of mob football[68].

---

67   Heraldry is a study of the coats of arms; the emblems of various important families, including the shield, crest and helm, supported either side by supporters (such as the lion and unicorn on the British royal family's coat of arms).

68   Football was played in Tudor England in a variety of different ways. Mob football is sometimes also referred to as village football or Shrovetide football, the latter being named after Shrove Tuesday, on or around when the game was often played. The game had been around for hundreds of years by then, the early rules being that – as long as you didn't commit murder or manslaughter – just about anything goes! In some versions, the winners were the team that got the ball to their own village. In another version, the winners were the one whose team kicked the ball into the other village's church! The balls were usually made of stuffed pig's bladder or of wood.

If you have never been in a position to witness such a game, Thomas, let me explain a little more.

Firstly, in a game of mob football, the word game is somewhat inaccurate. The teams are made up of two villages, so the word 'battle' or 'war' might be more appropriate. When I say villages, I mean villages, or the entirety of their inhabitants at the very least. There is no set number of people to a team. Each and every inhabitant of a village who is willing and able to take part may do so.

The pig's bladder ball may be kicked or carried or thrown. Those trying to gain control of the ball may also kick or carry or throw or punch or tackle the person with the ball... or any person in the way, come to that. Or any person in the opposite team they may wish to kick or carry or throw or punch or tackle. Or in their own team, if they bear a grudge and wish to settle old scores when no one is looking or does not care.

Weapons are not allowed, but who is to say that a walking stick or staff is a weapon, or a tool one has about one's person in the line of work, or a knife which one always carries in one's belt? To put it simply, the rules are few and far between, and may vary from village to village, referee to referee.

The two teams meet midway between the two villages. The referee declareth the game begun and the first team to land the ball back at an agreed place in their own village is declared the winner.

Now, this may well sound violent enough but imagine yourself in my position. Holding the ball as the villagers from Hamble Hooe and Hamble Stour descend upon me as one. What should I do? What DID I do? I threw the ball to John Rider.

I am not proud.

Do not judge me, Thomas.

An hour since, I tried telling myself that as instinctively as I'd caught the ball in the first place, I instinctively passed it on to John (who's catching of it was mighty fine, I might add). But, the truth be told, the reason for my ridding myself of the pig's bladder ball was plain and simple:

FEAR

No one may judge me unless they too have been faced by mob footballers. I suspect I could not be more afeared of a Spanish army armed to the teeth with the latest weaponry.

Not so good for poor John though.

With the villagers of Humble Hooe victorious, a celebration took place which included the defeated team of Humble Stour. Whereas, only hours before, nothing in the world seemed more important than each beating the other village at the game, now all is friendly once again. No one seems to bear a grudge.

It seems that the most common injury of a serious nature was broken limbs and there were plenty of these: arms, legs, fingers and toes. Then there were the noses. Few people escaped bruising, some badly, and there were people with

gappy-toothed smiles, cuts and lumps and bumps.[69]
Unfortunately, one of the people with a broken arm and leg and bruises and lumps and bumps and cuts and yet MORE lumps, was none other than poor John Rider.

---

69   In 1543, the following injuries after a game of football were mentioned: "*Sometimes their necks are broken, sometimes their backs, sometimes their legs, sometimes their arms, sometimes one part is thrust out of joint, sometimes the noses gush out with blood.*"

He is now in the care of a Mistress Cartwell, Humble Hooe's Wise Woman, who is well-known in the village for her herbal medicines and healing powers. Apparently, her mother was a Wise Woman[70] before her, as well as a botcher[71]. Most fortunately Mistress Cartwell's apothecary's box contains a piece of rope that was used to hang a man which she assures me, when applied to poor John's head, will help to ease the pain.[72]

"How bad do you consider Master John's condition to be?" I asked the old lady. I suspect that she may be as much as forty, Thomas![73]

"I was fortunate enough to get a sample of your friend's urine but an hour ago and have studied it closely,"[74] she replied.

"And?" I asked, trying to keep the worry from my voice.

"Having tasted it, I would say that I am hopeful he'll make a full recovery, given time.[75]"

I heaved a sigh of relief. "I have important matters to attend to, Miss Cartwell," I said, "but I would be extremely

---

70 Wise Women were local healers. Their remedies were a mix of genuinely useful herbs and concoctions, common sense and superstition.

71 A mender of old clothes.

72 Tudor medicine hadn't advanced much from medieval medicine and was still very basic. Pressing a hangman's rope to your head was, indeed, supposed to help head pain. If you had rheumatism, the recommended cure was to wear the skin of a donkey!

73 Only around 10% of people in Tudor England lived to be forty-years-old or over.

74 Tudor 'doctors' and 'healers' believe much could be told about a patient's condition just by looking at their urine.

75 Yes, as well as looking at and smelling urine, some healers also drank a little. Yerch!

grateful if I could leave him in your care. I will, of course, pay you for your trouble." I produced a coin and handed it to her.

Her eyes widened when she saw that it was half a crown[76].

"It will be my honour to look after your friend for as long as is necessary," she assured me.

I said my goodbyes to John, who groaned a great deal but wished me luck by name. We had managed to retrieve one of the horses – his stallion, Star – and Mistress Cartwell hath assured me that, should my mount return in my absence, she will be fed, stabled and watered until my return.

And so ended Mark's remarkable account.

---

76   Eight half-crowns made a pound (£) and many farm labourers would only earn between five and ten pounds a year.

Day 7

More people arrive daily and Master Tundy
now hath a piece of parchment laid out upon
his impressive desk of carved oak. He is aware
that I can read but not, I suspect, just how well.
I have also been trained in the art of reading
items *upside-down*, should I only glance them

from the wrong side of a desk. Lord Severn trained us well, whatever age we may be.

Master Tundy hath written a series of columns, listing the name of each guest, whether he hath his wife accompanying him, and the name or number of those he hath to attend him (if known). He also had letters and numbers allocated to each group.

"The numbers," said the steward, carefully watching my gaze, "refer to the bed chambers I have allocated them." The chambers themselves do not have numbered doors. "The letter, refers to the wing of the house. 'E' for east, 'W' for west…"

"And the 'C', Master Tundy?" I asked, not aware of there being a letter C anywhere upon the points of a compass.

"The main house, Thomas. The original house, where we are now. Where Lady Drayshire[77] herself hath her chamber."

I wasn't aware that 'main' or 'original'

---

77   The wife of an Earl is a countess, but is usually referred to as 'Lady' with the name of the Earldom after it – in this case, Drayshire.

began with 'C' either, and I am exceeding well educated for a boy of my age.

"For Central," said Master Tundy, as if he'd read my mind. "The 'C' is for 'central'."

I must be careful with the steward. He seemeth to be very good at understanding what people may be thinking!

Being a house of such magnitude, it will take me forever to learn the location of each room and the twist and turn of each corridor, but I do have a sense of the general layout. As is the latest style, it is in the form of a letter H[78]. The west wing (W) is the first line of the H, the central part of the house (C), which incorporates parts of a much older building, is the crossbar of the H, and the East Wing (E) the right-hand vertical.

The original Goldenhilt Hall was obviously

---

78 Another popular shape for the layout of Tudor houses was in the form of the letter E.

of timber-frame and wattle-and-daub construction[79]. At some stage, the additional wings had been added to the property in stone and, more recently still, much of it had been clad in brick, the very latest fashion[80]. At this stage, some very fine windows would also

---

79 Most Tudor homes weren't built of brick or stone but were timber-framed with the gaps between timbers filled by wattle and daub. Wattle is a woven lattice of strips of wood, and daub – with which the wattle is daubed/covered – is a thick layer made up of wet soil, clay, sand and even animal dung, often mixed with straw. This could dry to a smooth finish.
80 Tudor bricks are smaller and thinner than today's traditional house-brick and are of slightly pinker colour. They were handmade.

have been added[81] and, even more recently, I suppose, the staircase. The craftsmanship of the staircase is truly remarkable. I am used to staircases of stone, or simple, almost ladder-like construction. The staircase here is a marvel of wooden design. The walls lining the staircase are a mixture of wooden panelling – matching the staircase's boards, banister and newel posts[82] – and of white plaster.

---

81   Glass was expensive, so large widows were a way of showing off one's wealth. One of the most famous large-windowed Tudor buildings is Hardwicke Hall.

82   The wooden uprights supporting the bannister. Newel posts at the bottom of the stairs were usually the most ornately carved.

(Who knew I could get so excited over a stretch of steps?)

I have not much else to report. I am familiarising myself with the layout of the house while I can. Master Tundy expects much work of me, but seems fair.

Speaking of which, today I caught sight of The Lady Anna de Grieff,[83] the daughter of my host, the Earl of Drayshire, and she too seems fair, but in another way. (Her brother, Simon – the viscount – I am informed, is interested in

---

83   As the daughter of an earl, Anna is given the honorary title of 'The Lady Anna', always with a capital 'T'. Even in the middle of a sentence.

horses above all else. He is usually out riding and I have yet to glimpse him.) The Lady Anna is a most pretty girl. She was wearing a dress as green as her eyes. And, just to be clear upon the matter, her eyes are very green, like a cat's. (A cat with green eyes, that is. Ignore amber and blue-eyed cats.) I imagine that she must be not much older than myself. And I do imagine her. A great deal.

When we spoke, she smiled shyly. "Oh, so you are Lord Snoop's nephew," she said. "I am most pleased you're here to help old Rotundy!" For a moment, she looked aghast at having spoken aloud her nickname for the steward. Then she giggled. (Rotund means plump and, as I have stated previously, Master Tundy is indeed a little round about the middle!)

"It is a rare opportunity to visit such a grand home," I replied.

We passed a few more pleasantries, then went our separate ways.

Day 8

The greatest marvel I have yet laid eyes on in Goldenhilt Hall, this house of wonder, is the long gallery. With it vaulted ceiling of deeply moulded plaster, and a floor that runs the whole length of the house, with a window front and back, I've never seen anything like it. The steward took me there this morning.

"Pray, what is it for, Master Tundy?" I asked. "What is its purpose?"

"It hath many purposes. It demonstrates that my lord and master, the earl, hath the wealth and power to build such a fine room. It demonstrates his excellent taste in the most modern of ideas. It took many months to build and I can account for every penny of it,[84]" said the steward.

"It is a gallery for his lordship to display portraits of his most worthy ancestors." He

---

84   Keeping detailed household accounts was an important part of the steward's job.

nodded at the oil painting upon the wall, which were of some of the most owl-like people I have ever seen: big-eyed and small-beaked. I mean, *nosed*. "And it is a place for the ladies and gentlemen to walk and talk. For them to discuss business or gossip when the weather is deemed too poor to venture into the gardens. It is a place of exercise."

I found myself glancing at the steward's stomach. I rather suspect that he is not one for much exercise himself.[85]

We had reached the large window – stretching from waist-height to ceiling – at one end of the gallery. In the middle, made from stained glass, was the de Grieff family crest, with the turnip on its shield, and supported on one side by an eagle and by a hare on the other. With a stone surround, this vast window is made up of a number of sections, the diamond panes of glass held together in a latticework of lead holding them in place. The lower sections of window are hinged and can

---

85   Not that he would have been allowed to use the long gallery.

be opened.

Along with the basic layout of the house and garden, Lord Severn had supplied me with diagrams of a number of types of window. Why? Because different types of windows can be entered from the outside by different means: a latch lifted or the leading heated, when necessary, then bent back and the glass removed.

Fixed Light   Fixed Light

Mullion
Saddle Bar
Stanchion Bar
Transom
Mullion (section)
Turnbuckle (from above)
Handle (from side)
Casement (opening light)
Fixed Light

It is Lord Severn's belief that the more one knoweth about a subject, the better one is prepared to tackle it if and when the need arises. Especially if one is a boy and can fit through smaller gaps than a fully-grown spy!

The three most important rooms to me at present are all in the middle section of the house:

- the kitchens
- the steward's office
- the Great Hall, with its fine wood panelling, tapestries and even grander windows; its roof, with its carved beams, so high that there are no rooms above it.

The Great Hall is where the guests will congregate and be entertained. It is here that I shall eavesdrop on their conversations as best I can. Master Tundy's office is important because it containeth the name of each and every guest and their servants, and a set of keys to every room with a locked door.

As for the kitchens, this is where I hope to befriend as many servants as I can without suspicion. The cook himself is a man named

Garble, who hath the rare distinction of having but one arm. One-armed men are not unknown to me, but he is the first one-armed cook I have yet encountered! Fortunately, he hath an army of lesser cooks and helpers to assist him in his work.

He is more a shouter of orders than a dicer of vegetables! I say the word *army* advisedly for he runneth this huge kitchen like he's still in the army, though I doubt he was ever very senior in the ranks.

Despite his looking very like a hell-mouth

painting[86] and barking orders like an order-
barker – I cannot think of a better example
at present – he hath taken a shine to me and
seems a nice enough fellow.

---

86 Wall-painting in Christian churches often showed the entrance to
hell and all the horrors it contained, as a way of reminding people
what would happen if they sinned.

"How d'ya like old Ro?" he asked.

"I don't think I've met him," I replied.

"Tundy!" said Garble, his terrifying-looking face breaking into a toothy grin. "Rotundy! That's what we calls him. He must have a good pair of lungs, what with him shoutin' out orders all day!"

You're one to talk, I thought. But said nothing.

"The only time he ain't bellowin' is when he's making sure he hath more than his fair share of my fill!" he said, laughing again and sticking his stomach forward in a reasonable impersonation of the steward.

"More work, Garble, and less idle chatter," said a voice behind me. Master Tundy had appeared out of the shadows. None of us had heard him enter. So much for my spying skills, being alert at all times.

"You heard the man!" shouted Garble, as though his staff had been the ones receiving the telling off, when they'd been working away in silence. He picked up a carrot[87] and bit the end off with a loud

CRUNCH,

as if to remind the steward that, in the kitchen at least, HE is in charge.

---

87   Carrots weren't orange until the seventeenth century, so it's likely that the one Garble ate was a purple colour.

Tundy turned to me. "Done here, Snoop?" he asked.

"Yes, sire," I nodded.

On the way out, I bumped into a man I now know to be Scullion[88] the spit boy.[89] Remember Green, the man I met in the forest, clutching a dead wolf? The biggest man I had ever seen? The Wild Man of the Woods with the slate green eyes? The man I described as being the size of a small village and about as wide? The biggest human being I ever expected to see?

Scullion is

EVEN LARGER.

---

88 Scullion was a fifteeth century term for a servant with the most menial kitchen tasks. So it can't have been his actual name.

89 A spit boy was, more often than not, a fully-grown man whose job it was to turn the huge spit – on which there might be pretty much a whole pig or bullock or deer – in front of an open fire for hours on end. This would have been an exhausting job even without the heat of the fire. With the heat, it must have been almost unbearable. The fat dripping from the cooking animal would have been caught in a trough beneath.

"Sorry," I said, directly to his stomach, at my eye level.

High above my head, Scullion grinned like an oaf.

Day 12

I have been so busy with my duties, both for Master Tundy and for Lord Severn, that this is the first time I have had an opportunity to update this diary. Goldenhilt Hall is now filled with some of the most important and finely-dressed noblemen and women in the country. I cannot deny that I feel a certain thrill at being in their presence, but also feel that I am ready for the task ahead.

Suddenly the house is filled with colour. The laws of apparel mean that I have become used to being surrounded by fellow servants dressed in blue or drab brown.[90] And the hats. Some

---

90   The law of apparel (clothes) was also known as the sumptuary laws. There were strict rules about what someone in Tudor Britain could or could not wear based on their place in society. One could tell at a glance who was a labourer, merchant or gentleman, just by the cut and colour of their clothes. Only royalty could wear purple. The very rich and powerful wore black, because truly black dyes were very expensive. Red denoted happiness. More important servants wore blue. There were harsh punishments for those who wore clothes above their entitlement/place in society. It was another way of exerting control. Like most Tudor laws, they were there to protect the rich and the powerful.

of these hats have to
be seen to be believed.
I know it is not my
place, but some give
the impression of a noble
lord wearing a great
squashy loaf of bread
upon his head, a feather
jauntily placed on top!

Now that all the Lords
and Ladies have their
rooms, and have their retinues[91] to attend to
them, along with Goldenhilt's servants, my
daily tasks for Master Tundy have changed.
And, though I have less opportunity to go
here, there and everywhere, I have more
opportunities to lose myself amongst the
guests and to make myself useful in ways
where I can eavesdrop.

On my way to the servant stairs, I saw my
friend Mark Tolland once more.

---

91   A retinue is a group of advisers, assistants, or others accompanying
an important person.

"Is your master happy with the arrangements?" I asked, referring to Lord Mulberry.

"He is never happy with anything," said Mark, his voice low. "He claims the room too small and the bed too hard… when the room could stable all our horses and the bed would suit the fussiest princess! Lady Mulberry is more easily pleased but still highly strung."

"Any news of your friend, John Rider?" I asked. I had not forgot the account of the terrible football match!

"He should be well enough to return to Mulberry Manor by the week's end," said Mark, "but he will not be back to full strength for weeks to come."

He was about to say more, but I was distracted by a flash of green. The Lady Anna was slipping out into the garden. She looked troubled. Her face was flushed and her skin looked clammy. Her hair was less than perfectly arranged.

When the opportunity arose, I followed her into the night air with the stealth of a *[door hinge]*.[92]

---

92   I'm not sure door hinges are very stealthy. They certainly can't tiptoe. I suspect this is another of Thomas's coding errors but have NO IDEA what the actual word he intended might have been.

Goldenhilt Hall hath a more formal garden immediately surrounding the house itself, outside which is a deer park which, as the name suggesteth, is a park for deer. Or, to be even more specific, a park in which the Earl of Drayshire and his friends may hunt deer, which must be an easy enough sport, there being so many of them. Deer, that is, not friends of the Earl of Drayshire, though there be plenty of them also.

In the failing light, I could make out The Lady Anna heading for the maze. Mazes are the height of fashion, so there is little surprise that a house such as Goldenhilt would have one. I cannot imagine that the maze at Nonsuch is any finer![93]

---

[93] Nonsuch was one of the finest royal palaces ever built in Britain. A village was destroyed to make room for its construction by Henry VIII. It wasn't finished when he died in 1547. After his daughter Mary became Queen, she sold it to the Duke of Arundel in 1556 who then completed it. By the 1590s it was a royal palace again and remained so until King Charles II gave it to the Countess of Castlemaine in 1670. She had it pulled down in 1682 and sold it off, brick by brick to pay off a gambling debt. As well as being an amazing building, it is said to have had an amazing maze.

As well as her unsettled appearance,
there was something different in The Lady
Anna's manner of walking. Something out of
character. This is just the kind of behaviour I
have been trained to note and act upon, but I
was unable to follow her as I might have done
in most other circumstances. When she actually

entered the maze, it would have been madness to follow her in. Not only might I have become completely and utterly lost, but she could have turned back upon herself and walked into me at any time, and there was no convincing way I could have explained the reason for my presence.

Instead, I hid myself behind a conveniently situated shrub and, working alongside the similar principle that what goes up must come down, I satisfied myself in the knowledge that someone who enters a maze must come out again. I waited.

The Lady Anna reappeared sooner than I had expected but her transformation was noticeable. Though the same on the outside, she bore herself with more dignity. Her look of panic and uncertainty had been replaced with a look of fixed determination. A *grim* determination. It was as if her whole inner-self had transformed.

Whom had she met in there who made her behave so differently when departing, I wondered.

A lover?

A *Spanish* lover, perhaps?

Perhaps she was unknowingly being lured into some Spanish plot by a Spanish lad pretending to like her?

I decided not to follow The Lady Anna back to the house but to remain hidden behind the shrub and see who – if anyone else – left the maze.

I did not have to wait long, but what I saw – *who* I saw – has chilled me to the core. I can make no sense of it.

For the second person to leave the maze *was*

also The Lady Anna!

No, this is no error in my writing of the code. The person to leave the maze after The Lady Anna was…

HERSELF!

Had she somehow managed to re-enter the maze, unseen by me, by some different route? Surely that was not possible – and, anyhow, there would not have been enough time. And certainly not enough time for her to also change her clothing. This second Lady Anna was dressed differently to the first… but it was her without a doubt. She walked past my hiding place close enough for me to touch her. I would swear by Almighty God it was The Lady Anna… but how can this be?

I was about to follow her when I was interrupted by the kitchen boy Peter. Standing behind me, the shrub offered me no protection, and he did not even ask what on Earth I might be doing, for it was not his

place!⁹⁴

"Oh there you are, Master Snoop," he said, picking his nose and looking upon me with a what-are-you-up-to smile. "Master Tundy hath been calling for you."

---

94   'Not his place' as in not in Peter's place in the hierarchy of servants. His main job was to do as he was told!

Under any other circumstances, I might have been concerned that the steward had noticed my absence, but my mind was still reeling from what I had seen of The Lady Anna with mine own eyes.

It must be witchcraft.

Master Tundy was waiting for me in his office. With all the guests now here, he bid me to move about the Hall ensuring that everything was running as best as could be hoped for. And to report back. He sought perfection.

I cannot believe my luck! Lady Margaret P— (whose name rhymes with turtle[95]) had asked the same of me, to be *her* eyes and ears; and, thus, the eyes and ears of Lord Severn. And now, whether he knows it or not, the steward hath given me reason to be anywhere about Goldenhilt Hall without question! What spy could ask for more?

95　In medieval times, a number of bestiaries were produced. A bestiary was a highly illustrated book – a compendium of beasts – which listed names and descriptions of animals both real and imagined (but written as though all were real). This included the Aspidochelone, sometime described as a GIANT TURTLE so big that it was mistaken for an island! Such books remained popular in Tudor times, though knowledge of true natural history was growing.

Day 13

I dreamed of The Lady Anna last night and of her twin. For, of course, once I had the chance to clear my mind and think logically, that can be the only conclusion: that there are TWO of them.

I don't mean that they are literally twins, or sisters, even – though, on the one occasion I saw them, their likeness was extraordinary – but that there is The Lady Anna and one other who is her likeness. A double, like a reflection in a mirror given life. But who is this other Lady Anna? And what does this mean?

Though still keeping my eyes and ears open for anything else out of the ordinary, it seemeth obvious to me that the MOST extraordinary thing I have encountered since my arrival is the two Annas, so I shall make her the centre of my investigation.

Down in the kitchen, I found the one-armed Garble shouting out his orders as usual, and his small army of staff busying themselves like the worker bees in my father's skeps[96].

I greeted him with a wave of the arm as though sent on an errand and with no time to delay, and slipped out into the gardens from a rear entrance.

Despite the early hour, I was not alone. Two men I knew to be Lord Roebuckle and the Most Noble Thomas Casement, Duke

---

96   Tudor beehives were called basket hives or skeps. They were usually conical and made of braided straw, and kept in 'bee boles', alcoves especially built into the south-facing walls of big houses. Bee-keeping was a popular pastime in Tudor Britain. Interestingly, honey bees were not black-and-yellow-striped as we know today, but black.

of Hampton, were deep in conversation of a seemingly relaxed nature. I was able to catch a snatch of conversation:

"—and, as we passed through Laughton, the wheel shaft of our carriage broke clean in two!" said the duke.

"And the duchess[97]?" asked a concerned Roebuckle, "She was unharmed?"

The duke snorted. "She was less flustered than I! But the reason I tell you this is that our unscheduled stop resulted in my witnessing some most extraordinary entertainment of which I have heard but never seen with mine own eyes. Until now!"

---

97   A duke's wife has the title of duchess.

He paused for effect.

"Pray tell," said Roebuckle obligingly.

"Why, it is the fine art of shin-kicking[98], where two worthy opponents kick each other in the shins with as much force as possible. It had been our intention to take sanctuary in a hostelry whilst repairs to our carriage were

---

98   No, this isn't one of Thomas's mistakes in writing in code. Shin-kicking was, indeed, a Tudor sport. Ouch!

undertaken but a crowd had gathered outside,"
the duke continued. "Our arrival coincided
with the local shin-kicking champion, one Watt
Thatcher, being challenged by a certain John

Thatcher – no relation – from another shire[99]. This we learned from one of the many people circling the two shin-kickers to create an impressive crowd. There was much cheering for the local man with cries of 'Watt! Watt! Watt!' 'We normally cry

---

99 In Tudor times, and before, many people gained their family name from the profession that the men folk were mainly involved in. The original Thatchers would have thatched rooves. Tylers tiled. The Baker family would have baked, and so on. This is why Smith is such a common name: because there were so many types of smith (people who worked with metal): blacksmith, goldsmith, arrowsmith, bladesmith, coppersmith, locksmith and – later – gunsmith, to name just a few.

'Thatcher!' your grace[100],' some jangler[101] in the crowd explained to me, mightily excited by proceedings, 'but that would not be of much use on this occasion!'"

"The sport of the common man," Lord Roebuckle commented. "Rather different from our own pursuits."

"It seemed to me that the challenger, John, had an unfair advantage because he appeared to be wearing special boots with metal attached to the toes," said the Duke of Hampton, "Every kick from both man was accompanied by an 'Oooo!' or an 'Ahhh!' from large portions of the crowd. To say that it looked painful would be like saying that sitting in the middle of a roaring fire is a little hot for one's behind!"

Both men roared with laughter.

"And who, pray, won, your grace?"

"The eventual victor was the local man, Watt Thatcher. His opponent, metal-toe-

---

100 Your grace is the correct 'form of address' when speaking to a duke, in the same way 'my lord' or 'your lordship' would be when addressing a lord.
101 The Tudor slang for chatterbox: someone who spoke a lot!

capped boots or not, lay rolling on the ground clutching – thy guessed it – his shins! The crowd was delighted, shouting abuse, the most polite of which was 'Cod's head[102]!'"

---

102   A blockhead. In other words: an idiot.

"Extraordinary!"

"I must confess that, despite my initial reservations, I found it a most exhilarating sport to watch, but the duchess was less impressed. 'It's just two men kicking each other,' she reasoned, but I do not expect a woman to appreciate the finer art of such a sport."

And that was the full extent of what I could hear without risk of being called an eavesdropper.

So what did I learn from this of possible importance? That the shaft in the duke's carriage broke. Could this have been a deliberate attempt to harm him, or an attempt to prevent him from reaching Goldenhilt? Or was this merely an excuse for the duke to pay a visit to a hostelry where he might have a secret liaison with a Spanish spy? Or did the shaft simply break because it was an accident? So many questions, but the information stored away: the Duke and Duchess of Hampton had a seemingly unplanned stop in Laughton.

The remaining people I saw about the

gardens were servants, either of the Earl of Drayshire's household or of our noble visitors. I caught up with my friend Mark Tollman – victim of mob football, a game more violent still than shin-kicking – and we walked together along a gravel path.

Just then a very

LARGE

shadow was cast over the pair of us then gone.
It was Scullion.

"Woah!" said Mark Tolland in surprise. "Did
I imagine that, or did an OGRE just pass us
by?"

I grinned. "That is Scullion the spit-boy,"
I said. "He is mighty tall, is he not?"

Mark shook his head in
disbelief. "Tall?" he said.
"*Tall?* If he were any
larger, he would have
to be declared a
separate country
in his own
right!"

I wished Mark a good day, and moved on.

I caught a glimpse of the spit-boy in the herb garden. I was surprised to see him carefully pull up a particular plant by thumb and forefinger, with great care for a man with fists like hams.

Now I entered the maze. I had every confidence that I would not get lost for two reasons:

Firstly, I had studied the single route to the centre and out again on the map I had been provided, showing the layout of the house and garden.

Secondly, I had overheard a trick as to how to defeat it. If I kept my left hand touching the left-hand hedge wall as I walk around it – even when I took the wrong path, reach a dead-end and had to turn round – then it would eventually lead me to the centre.

I wanted to see if the maze could yield any clues as to the mystery of the two Lady Annas.

Day 14

Another day hath passed since I have had the
opportunity to update events in this diary. I
was interrupted by a commotion last night
as I was writing up my observations.
It was late at night and I was writing
by candlelight in my chamber when
a servant, Stephen – a boy of about
my age but not my birth[103] – burst in,

---

103   Thomas Snoop was the nephew of a lord, remember. Stephen must
      have been a servant from a more ordinary background.

without so much a knock or a by-your-leave,
urging me to find Master Tundy that instant
because there had been a sighting of a ghost.

Yes, a ghost!

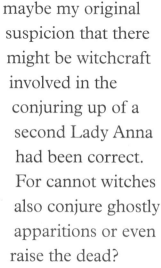

My first thought was that
maybe my original
suspicion that there
might be witchcraft
involved in the
conjuring up of a
second Lady Anna
had been correct.
For cannot witches
also conjure ghostly
apparitions or even
raise the dead?

I asked the servant
Stephen to tell me
more as we both hurried to the
door, but he was poorly informed. Apparently
the earl himself had stumbled upon him,
demanding the whereabouts of Master Tundy,
who was neither in his chamber nor his
steward's office and was nowhere to be found.

(I stored this piece of information with interest, despite the matter in hand.)

His lordship was saying that not one but TWO guests had witnessed a ghost upon the staircase and that he required his steward this instant!

As I ran in search of Master Tundy, I remembered a piece of advice given to me by Lord Severn, *'Let the clergy deal with God. We deal in what is before us. I have never encountered something seemingly inexplicable that cannot be explained by Earthly means.'*

I found the steward in the kitchen. He had prepared himself a *[small squeal]*[104] which was laid out on a pewter platter[105] before him. He looked somewhat guilty at being discovered!

---

104   Another coding error! A small meal, more likely.
105   Pewter is a grey metal alloy which can be polished to a silver shine. A pewter platter (plate) is not as posh as a silver one.

What was it Garble the cook had said? *'The only time he ain't bellowin' is when he's making sure he hath more than his fair share of my fill!'*

I quickly told him what had happened and we hurried to the staircase where the Earl of Drayshire was waiting for him.

Standing at the steward's side, I soon learned what was said to have occurred:

One of the guests, the Lady Mulberry, had turned the bend in the staircase, having been walking up from below, and caught a glimpse of a shadowy figure walking down the stairs ahead of her, then *walking through a wall*. I've little doubt what her ladyship saw would have been put down to tiredness and a trick of the flickering candlelight were it not for the fact that the Duchess of Hampton had been coming down the stairs at the same time. She had caught sight of a figure walking just ahead of her on the landing and starting down the stairs but when, moments later, the duchess

herself had reached the stairs, ***the figure had gone*** and the only person there was Lady Mulberry coming up them, who let out a cry! "Where are the ladies now, my lord?" asked Master Tundy.

"I have put them together in a side chamber," said the earl. "Lady Mulberry is quite hysterical and the Duchess of Hampton is calming her. They could not be less alike. The duchess has no time for fingle-fangles.[106] She is very much a no-nonsense person, for which I thank the Lord. Were both ladies hysterical, I suspect we'd wake the household."

The last thing the earl wanteth, with the Hall full of noble guests, is fear and rumour about a haunting!

"What would you have me do, my lord?" asked Master Tundy.[107]

"Do?" asked the Earl of Drayshire. He had been in such a hurry to call upon his steward but, now that he'd found him, he didn't seem sure how to proceed. "*Do*? You have been given the task of ensuring that the week runs smoothly and that my guests are happy. I

---

106 Tudor slang for 'trifles', things of little value or importance.
107 As with most fine Tudor households, much of the day-to-day running of the property would be at the bidding of the lady of the house, in this case the countess. The steward would probably have taken more orders, suggestions and requests from her rather than her husband, though he was ultimately 'in charge'.

would have you sort this!"

With that, he turned and went up the stairs to his chamber and, presumably, to his bed and to sleep.

The steward turned to me. "Apparently, we are to sort this, young Snoop," he said. "You see if you can encourage the ghost to reappear.

If it does, plead with it to *dis*appear again and never to come back and upset our guests. I, meanwhile, shall speak to the ladies, beseech them to say nothing to anyone but their husbands, and ensure that they are escorted to their beds."

"Why me, Master Tundy?" I asked.

"Why you what, Thomas?"

"Why am I the one to deal with the ghost, Master Tundy? I know nothing of ghosts or ghouls or spectres."

"I thought that should be obvious," replied the steward, his grinning face half hidden in the flickering candlelight. "I know nothing about them either, but I do know how to calm distraught guests, and it is best to employ my energies where my expertise lies!"

And that is why, at some ungodly hour at the dead of night, I was walking up and down the wooden staircase wondering what I should be doing.

I stood at the bottom of the stairs looking up, wondering roughly where Lady Mulberry had been when she had seen – or thought she

had seen – the apparition ahead of her. I wish
I could have interviewed her personally rather
than hear the story second-hand, but that is, of
course, not possible.

I noted the position of the window,
wondering if she might somehow have seen

an image of a portrait somehow reflected in candlelight in the glass and back onto the wall…but there were no portraits on the stairwell walls and, more importantly, coming down, the Countess had also seen a figure disappear.

I tapped every inch of panelling and plaster along the wall in the turn of the staircase, pressing my ear to the wood as I went. My excitement mounting, there was nothing more I could do without daylight, so I returned to my chamber, blew out my *[sandal]*[108] and fell into a deep sleep.

---

108   Yes, he must have meant *candle*, surely?

The following morning – in other words, *this* morning – there was no gossip about ghosts or apparitions from the servants, which was impressive. Those who had witnessed the previous night's antics must have been ordered to hold their tongues, and have done so. I wondered whether Lady Mulberry and the Duchess of Hampton would be as discreet or, when they arose at a later hour, the haunting would become the talk of the guests.

I was up at dawn and slipped out into the garden. The grass beneath my feet was wet with dew but my eyes were upward, studying the back of the Hall. I could make out the large window that illuminates the staircase and yes – there! – that was what I was looking for. It was so difficult to spot at first that it would only be visible for someone really looking out for it, such as myself!

To call it a window would be misleading for, today, our windows have glass. It was more like a glassless window of a castle or, better still, more like a hole through which one might fire

an arrow! But I suspect that this oblong[109] hole – the size of four missing bricks or so – has a very different purpose: to give light and air to a priest hole!

---

109   Rectangular.

A priest hole is a tiny secret room in which Catholics hide their priest if the authorities come calling. The entrance is disguised, and its window – if it has one – must be also. I believe what the lady and the duchess saw was not a ghost walking through a wall but a robed priest disappearing through a secret entrance to the hole…

…which means that Lord Severn's intelligence was right and that there are Roman Catholic plotters at the Hall, but not as guests. *It is William de Grieff, the Earl of Drayshire himself. He continues to follow the old faith!*

This is the most extraordinary piece of information. The earl is seen as a close friend of the king. If I am right – and with a priest hole built in the newest part of his house I cannot see how this cannot be so – then he is a Catholic. But does that mean that he is in league with the Spanish against King Edward? It is *this* part that I must be sure of before I report my findings.

From last night's investigation of the

panelling up the stairs, confirmed by today's positioning of the tiny window, I was now confident that I knew the priest hole's location.

I decided that I must investigate this further – under the cover of darkness – as soon as the opportunity arose.

Once I realised the significance of my discovery, I also realised that I must tell Master Tundy nothing of it. After all, the Earl of Drayshire is his master and who knows – he may also be in league with the Spanish at his master's bidding! But why, if he knew about the priest hole, would he ask *me* to investigate the ghost and risk its discovery, rather than saying that he would do it, and thus be sure to keep it secret?

Then it occurred to me. It might be more important for him to encourage the ladies to say nothing… and he simply thinks of me as an assistant, and not a highly trained spy! He expected me to *find* nothing, in turn.

So I was decided. I would tell Master Tundy that our ghostly visitor had left no trace.

Enough of this. I must now return to another equally extraordinary set of events which occurred yesterday, which I had been in the process of writing up last night when Stephen had burst into my room and matters had taken such a sudden turn.

I had reached the point when I had entered the maze. I used the trick of keeping my left-hand to the left hedge and soon found myself in the centre. I wasn't sure what, if anything, I'd find…

but it certainly wasn't The Lady Anna herself.

I am not sure which of us was more surprised. She or I! My heart started beating like a barber's drum.[110] She had been seated at a small stone bench but jumped to her feet on my arrival.

"Lady Anna!" I said.

She looked at me, clearly having no idea who I was. She somehow looked both frightened and relieved at the same time.

"Good morrow," she said.

"'Tis I, Thomas Snoop," I said.

"Of course," she said. "You are here with…?"

---

110 Tudor barbers didn't just cut hair. They also carried out basic surgery and were dentists too. To 'drum up trade' their assistant or apprentice would beat a drum at markets and fairs, but the drum-beats had another purpose: to try to block out the screams of the patients having their teeth pulled. There were no anaesthetics!

"I work here, m'lady," I said. "With Master Tundy, the steward. I'm Lord Snoop's nephew."

"Of course," she said, a second time. "Then... Then why are you in the maze?"

I had been studying The Lady Anna de Grieff as we spoke, not with a casual eye but with that of a trained professional. I looked particularly at her earlobes, eyes and hands – those parts of a body which are hardest to disguise. And it was her hands which gave her away. They were rough, not smooth.

The discovery made my heart skip a beat. This young lady who stood before me now was an imposter. She was so like The Lady Anna but was *not* The Lady Anna.

"I was asked by Master Tundy to familiarise myself with the maze, your ladyship," I lied, "in case any of your father's noble visitors should become lost and require assistance in finding their way out."

"Good," said the false Lady Anna. "That... That is a good idea."

Suddenly, she burst into tears. Throwing

herself back onto the bench, she buried her head in her hands, her body wracked with sobbing.

I do not know if I would have dared touch the real Lady Anna, but I found myself putting my hand upon this lady's back as she leaned forward. "Don't cry, mistress," I said. My mind was working double time.

"I don't know if I can keep this up, Thomas," she said.

"Keep what up?" I asked, innocently.

"The lies. The games. The pretences," she sobbed. "It was never really a game to me but

now I feel I am the boar in their lordships' hunt!"[111]

"I don't understand, Lady Anna," I said.

The false Lady Anna turned to look at me with her beautiful green eyes. "I am not The Lady Anna," she said.

I tried to look suitably shocked. "You're not?" I said. "Then who are you?"

"Mary," she said, "Mary Wood. I live in forest yonder." She nodded in its direction. That *wa*s a surprise. She, a local peasant girl?

She took my hand in hers and squeezed it tight. We sat like that, side by side for a while, in silence but for her sobbing. I have been trained to know that silence is an excellent way of getting those who wish to talk to talk. To fill the gap.

It worked.

"I have to tell someone, or I shall burst!" she blurted out, letting go of my hand. Her accent was no longer that of The Lady Anna's

---

111 Wild boar were often hunted in woods and forests by nobles on horseback.

but of a country girl. And she told me her extraordinary tale.

A few months ago, The Lady Anna was out riding in this forest with her brother, the viscount Simon, when her horse was startled and bolted, and she was thrown to the ground. There were no bones broken, but she was shaken and sore. Mary's father found Anna and took her into their cottage to allow her to rest, whilst her brother seemed far more concerned about the missing horse and had ridden off in search of it.

Mary's family, the Woods, who laboured in the forest as woodcutters, charcoal-burners[112], and the like, could not have been kinder. As they tended to the noble young lady, they could not fail to notice how alike she was in appearance to their very own Mary! When Jane Wood, Mary's mother, who had not been at home when the accident occurred,[113] entered their home, even she mistook The Lady

---

112 A charcoal burner made charcoal from burning wood in special kilns or charcoal piles.

113 A wife was not only responsible for the house and garden, she would also have helped her husband with tough labouring in the fields and maybe even selling (as well as buying) at the market.

Anna for her own daughter, at first!
The long and the short of it was that The Lady
Anna returned to the Woods' hovel numerous times
in the weeks that followed, striking up a friendship
with Mary in particular, during which time Mary
taught her many of the country ways, and The
Lady Anna told Mary of her world: of the ways
of a young lady in a fine house and how she
had to behave.

It was *The Lady Anna* who had the idea of their switching places. Mary never would have dared suggest such a thing. Over the weeks that followed, *The Lady Anna* would visit Mary and train her in the ways of speech, deportment and etiquette until she thought Mary was ready to put it to the test.

One morning, she arranged for her brother Simon to meet her in the forest after riding, but it was Mary who met him in Anna's guise. They spoke awhile and Simon commented that Anna – really being Mary – was behaving a little oddly, but he did not for one moment imagine that he was not with his own sister… until Anna came out of hiding from behind a tree and revealed all! "You're alike as two clover!" he gasped.[114]

---

114 Today, we might say "as alike as two peas in a pod" but this phrase, though Tudor, didn't appear in print until 1580, in a play by John Lyly.

Two days ago, after going out riding with his sister, Simon de Grieff returned to Goldenhilt Hall with Mary disguised as Anna at his side. He would be there to guide and advise her in a strange house with people she did not know. The game was to see if Mary could last the rest of the day as The Lady Anna without being found out.

Here, Mary Wood stopped her tale. She had composed herself during the relating of it, and no longer had so much as a tear in the eye.

"So what happened, Mary?" I asked. "Are you not aware of the dangers of what you've done?"

"Aware?" said Mary, her eyes darting about nervously. "I know that I am in danger, but of what dangers do *you* speak?"

I wasn't about to say, 'of being mistaken for a spy and thrown into the Tower'[115], though that was a possibility. Instead, I said, "The laws of apparel. If any of these fine ladies or gentlemen were to discover that you are not one of them—"

She gave a most unladylike snort. "I have faced greater dangers than that! This was

NEVER

my idea and then… then…"

"And then, what, Mary?" I asked. "What happened next?"

"I witnessed something I was not supposed to see or hear. And two men came after me…"

"And what did you see?"

She looked at me, I suspect wondering whether she could trust me. Whether she had already said too much. And what did she see? An ordinary boy, sympathetic and ready to listen.

---

115   The Tower of London. Originally built as a castle by William the Conqueror, it became a prison to many people accused of treason over the centuries.

"I saw a very wide man. At least, he looked like a man but I'm sure I heard him being called by a woman's name."

"Can you recall the name?" I asked.

"I could under normal circumstances… I could if I hadn't knocked myself out! All I distinctly remember is being surprised that it was a *lady's* name and not a lord's," she said.

It was complicated enough having two Annas loose about the house, but a woman disguised as a man? Or a man with a woman's name?

This time, I took her hand. "Tell me, Mary," I said. "What exactly did you see?"

BEING AN EYE-WITNESS ACCOUNT OF EVENTS
AT GOLDENHILT HALL
BY MARY WOOD (IN THE GUISE OF THE LADY
ANNA DE GRIEFF)

AS TOLD TO THOMAS SNOOP.

Simon de Grieff could not be with me at all times, so I had to walk about the house of Goldenhilt as if it were my own home, with all the confidence of a daughter and a real lady. Many noblemen would bow or nod and introduce themselves in passing, and I would smile and nod and curtsey, and say a few oft-rehearsed words and phrases.

Sometimes, I would lose my nerve and try to avoid company, though I knew that simply staying in my chamber would have displeased Anna, and might have aroused suspicion with her father.

That evening, I turned down a corridor where two gentlemen were deep in conversation at the far end, walking toward me. Their voices were little more than a whisper and they looked uneasy. I felt both uncomfortable with their manner and nervous that I may not be able to maintain my pretence, so ducked into a doorway.

As they walked past, the thinner one slipped a folded piece of paper into the hand of the other, much wider, man, calling him by a woman's name. The wider man then spoke the words that chilled me to the bone: "Then we must kill him, in the name of Rome!" he said. I let out an involuntary gasp, giving away my hiding place. Two pairs of eyes turned towards me and looked deep into my soul. I ran out into the corridor and fled. The thinner man, who had passed the note, went to follow, but I heard the other say, "Let her go. We'll deal with her presently."

I fled to The Lady Anna's room but then it occurred to me that this might be the first place the men would look, so I hid in a variety of different places, but didn't feel safe in any of them. This place is not my home. 'Tis a different WORLD. I did not know what to do. I kept to unlit rooms and corridors, always turning back to see if I was being followed... which is how I ran into a low beam of a doorway. The next thing I knew, I awoke on the floor, my mind befuddled and confused. Getting to my feet, much of what had happened came back to me. Later I realised that there were gaps in in my memory – like dropped stitches in knitting[116] – such as forgetting the actual woman's name the one man called the other. Even now it is there just out of reach, like a moth on the other side of glass... I knew to keep moving. Had I been the real Lady Anna it might have been easy. As it was, I thought I best find Simon de Grieff, and tell him what had happened.

Whilst looking for Simon, I sought the safety of others. Surely no one would dare try to do me harm with so many witnesses about? Then, when simply walking from one room to another, my arm was grabbed by the thinner of the two men. His fingers dug deep into my flesh.

"I don't know what you think you heard, child," he hissed, "but we need to have a conversation. Alone."

---

116 In Tudor times, knitting really took off. When Henry VIII's daughter, Queen Elisabeth 1, became queen she made changes to the Laws of Apparel/the Sumptuary Laws, requiring every male over six to wear a knitted hat on Sundays and Holy Days. Failure to do so could result in a LARGE FINE. (This all tied in with England's wool industry, and protected the jobs of the cap-makers!)

This had been a mistake on his part for the corridor where I first encountered him was unlit, and he and the taller man were both in deep shadow. Now I could see him clearly and will certainly recognise him if I ever see him again, something which I would not be able to do with the other!

The second mistake was that he DIDN'T expect a refined lady, such as Anna, to have my strength from

working in the woods! I pulled myself free AND stamped on his foot at the same time. He was so surprised, that he didn't have time to react. I hurried out into the garden and to the maze, where it had been agreed – long before disaster struck and our changing places had been a 'game' – that the real Lady Anna and I should swap back to our original [bowls].[117]

---

117   Roles. He must have meant roles.

When The Lady Anna heard what had happened to me, she was outraged on my behalf. She wanted to go and tell her father and have him confront them there and then. The problem was, though, neither she nor I know who 'they' are... and for me to return with her to try to identify them would have caused problems of its own. So, rather than return home to my family as planned, she bid me go wait in the gatehouse whilst she found her brother Simon and they decided what to do.

I spent the night there, but neither returned. So, today, I hid in the maze, feeling safer amongst the myriad of passages, dead-ends and false turns.

I had, of course, witnessed Mary disappearing into the maze and the true Lady Anna leaving it. But, since then, I have discovered the priest hole and the true likelihood that The Lady Anna's father, the Earl of Drayshire, himself is very much involved in some Catholic plot. What a state of affairs!

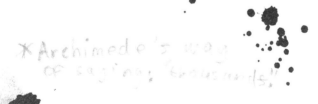

Archimede's way of saying; thousands!!

Day 16

Such a calamity hath befallen Goldenhilt Hall that I barely know where to begin. It is taking every ounce of my training to try to report matters in the order in which they occurred.

I decided that, until I could somehow find a way to get Mary Wood to identify the men who threatened her, without putting her in danger, there was some useful research I could do of my own.

Firstly, I could eliminate the names of all those who do not fit the physical description she gave of the two men, incomplete though these were. Of those remaining, I could then see if I could find any with woman-sounding names. If only there were a Lord Gertrude or a Marquis of Lucy!

To do this, I would need the list of all the guests and their allocated bedrooms, kept in Master Tundy's office. We often referred[118] to it, but I needed time to take it away and study it in detail. My opportunity arose when I found the office unattended.

Closing the door quietly behind me, I went over to Master Tundy's desk, and sat in his chair. Next to it, by the wall, was a fine locked chest, in which there were a number of drawers. The fine art of lock-picking is not a skill I have mastered, so it is fortunate that I know where he keepeth the key: in a

118 *Referred to* as in 'looked at it for information', not *referred to* as in 'talked about'.

small puzzle box[119] in the drawer of his desk. Fortunately, Master Tundy had shown me the solution, so I was able to open the box… and found it empty! It was then I noticed that *the key was already in the lock of the chest*.

---

119   A puzzle box is a box which appears to have no lid. It can only be
      opened by sliding, pressing or turning various pieces of wood into
      the correct positions in the correct order. A novelty or game, they
      can also make a satisfying hiding place for small objects.

This was most unlike Master Tundy. I had never known him leave it in there before. I was puzzling over this fact when I distinctly heard a groan.

I FROZE.
I WAS NOT ALONE
IN THE ROOM.

There it was again. Another groan. And equally unnatural.

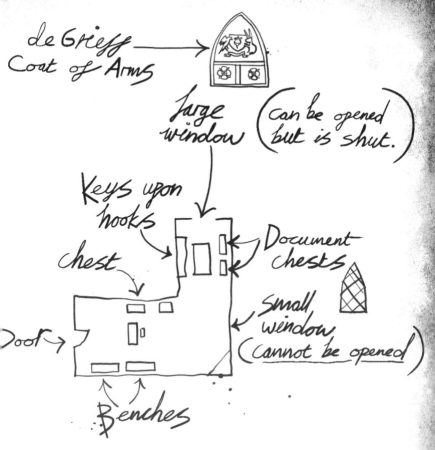

At this point, I should include a sketch showing the layout of the office. Once again, please forgive my poor penmanship.

As I hope my illustration at the very least portrays, it is an L-shaped room. I was by the desk which faces the door. The groan came from the other part of the L. It came from beneath the table. It came from Master Tundy.

He was lying in a pool of his own blood.

He had a dagger protruding from his stomach.

I knelt down beside him, lifting his head in my arms and holding it in my lap.

"Master," I said. "Master. Who did this to you?" I found that I was shaking.

He looked pleadingly into my eyes and tried to speak, but his lips could not form words. He groaned again and then managed to lift his right arm and point. But at what? The bottom of the table? I lowered my head to the level of his eyes and followed his gaze. "Who did this?" I said, realising that I was sobbing now. No training had prepared me for this.

Then I saw where Master Tundy's trembling finger was pointing. At the window. The window where, in the middle, picked out in stained glass, was the de Grieff coat of arms, with the eagle, the hare and the turnip.

Exhausted, his arm fell to the bloodied stone-flagged floor, his eyes closed and his head lolled to one side in my lap. My legs were sticky with his blood.

I had to call for help and I had to inform the Earl of Drayshire, his being the master of Goldenhilt Hall… but everything also seemed to point to *his being at the very heart of this dreadful plot.*

Having run into the corridor and called for the nearest servant to find the earl, his master,

with a matter of urgency, I quickly ran to the chest, opened it, pulled out the list, hid it beneath my garments, shut the lid, and then ran back to poor Master Tundy's side.

A few moments later, Anthony Barnaby, the master's secretary, strode into the room. "What matter is so urgent that –?" He stopped mid-sentence when he saw Master Tundy, dagger

sticking from his stomach. And all that blood.

He hurried over and put his fingers to Tundy's neck. "I feel his heartbeat," said Barnaby. "Master Tundy yet lives. Stay with him. Do not pull out the dagger, and I will summon assistance. Let no one else enter." He dashed from the room, pulling the door shut behind him.

After that was a whip-wind of activity. Master Tundy was carried from the room on a board, the floor was cleaned and the office locked. I was taken to see William de Grieff, Earl of Drayshire, in his own bed chamber.

He sat in a chair by the window. I could not take my eye off the stained glass crest, and kept thinking of Master Tundy's pointing finger. A finger of accusation.

We were alone. No servants. No one but he and I.

"Ah, Thomas Snoop," said the master of Goldenhilt Hall. He was dressed in finery, his clothes woven with gold thread, his fingers studded with rings, including the signet with which he stamped his seal[120], a fine hat upon his head.

---

120   Once written, a letter would be folded and sealed shut with melted sealing wax (often red). This was in the days before envelopes. To identify who the letter was from, and to show that it was authentic, the sender could then use his signet ring to make an impression of his coat of arms in the wax before it dried solid. If the seal was broken before it reached its intended recipient, it would show that the letter had already been read or tampered with.

At his secretary's instruction, I had changed my blooded clothes and washed the blood from my skin, so as not to alarm any passing guests. But I had also been told to be prompt about it.

"Lord Drayshire," I said, with head bowed[121].

"This is a terrible, terrible affair," said his lordship, "and at a most unfortunate time."

I wondered if there was ever a fortunate time to be stabbed?

"Will Master Tundy live?" I asked.

The earl stroked his neatly-trimmed grey beard. "That I cannot answer, Thomas," he said, "but I can tell you that, if he hath a chance of survival, he is in the best pair of hands to ensure that he does."

And if he does, I thought, *then he can name you as his attempted murderer*.

"I pray that he does, my lord," I said.

"We all do[122]," said the Earl of Drayshire. "Before I say any more, I have something to show you." He unfastened the top of his doublet[123] and pulled out a pendant strung on

---

121 Although his actual name is William de Grieff and his actual title is the Earl of Drayshire, he should be greeted as Lord Drayshire. Confusing, or what?

122 As Christians, praying to God for many things – happiness in marriage, success in battle, a bountiful crop – was vitally important.

123 A doublet was a type of jacket, popular with the wealthy and well-to-do.

an ornate chain of alternating gold and silver links. "Look," he said. "Look closely."

I looked. It was carved of bone in the shape of a rabbit poking its head out of a gap between parted grass. It had a toothy smile that reminded me of my father's servant, Hogg.

I felt a little leap inside my chest, which was lead-heavy at the thought of Master Tundy.

"I believe you have one such – er – trinket of your own," he said.

I did not know what to say. I realised that my breathing had quickened.

"A gift from Lady Margaret P—" he added, naming the lady with the unspellable name which, I think, rhymes with hurtle[124]. "To wish you luck."

If I were the kind of boy whose jaw dropped in surprise when surprised, my jaw would have dropped in surprise. "You…? You…?" I began.

---

124   As in two knights hurtling towards each other on horses, at a jousting tournament, trying to knock the other off theirs with a lance. (Tudor King Henry VIII was badly injured in a joust.)

"Yes," said the earl and then, in case I thought he'd somehow stolen the pendant from the Lady Margaret P— and was trying to trick me, he said the secret word to identify himself as working with Lord Severn, and I gave the appropriate response. (Writing in code or not, I am not so foolish as to write either here. I would have to be a real fopdoodle[125] to do that!)

So I was wrong. I had believed that no-one in Goldenhilt Hall knew that I was a spy, when its master knew all along!

He pointed to a stool. "Sit," he said. "And tell me all you know."

And so I did, doing my best to leave nothing out.

_____

125   No, not one of Thomas Snoop's coding errors, but Tudor slang for 'simpleton' or 'idiot'.

When I had finished, we sat in silence for a while whilst his lordship digested the information I had provided.

"So I was the one you suspected above all others?" he said, smiling without mirth.

"Yes, my lord," I said. "I… I…am sorry."

"Do not apologise," said his lordship. "You have no reason to, Snoop. You followed the evidence and it pointed towards me."

"What of the priest hole?" I asked.

"It was inspired by a priest hole but that is not its function," he replied. "You will gather that I have the confidence of the King. This gathering of nobles, for example, is an opportunity for us to discuss important matters away from the court and prying eyes of foreign ambassadors and the like. The room – the priest hole, as thy thought it – is a repository for the most secret of documents and, should it ever become necessary, the hiding of personages that need not concern you… but what puzzles me more is the window in the steward's office. If not pointing at the coat of arms, what was my poor, faithful

Roger Tundy trying to tell you?"

I produced Master Tundy's list of noble visitors and unfolded it.

"The answer lies in here, my lord. I'm sure of it," I said. "If we could just find someone with a womanly-sounding name and…"

"With the name Glass or Window-Pane!" said the earl. "I doubt our chances. I feel that we should have everyone assemble in the Great Hall, bring this Mary Wood girl in, disguised to look very different to her usual self and my daughter, and see if something – *any*thing – jolts her memory into remembering some minor detail that helps her identify the treacherous plotters who threatened her!"

"Her memory seems hazy," I said, "and I fear time may be against us, your lordship. For them to have attacked Master Tundy, knowing that he – or his body – might soon be discovered…"

"Yes. That's true–" he began, but I interrupted him.

"My Lord!"

"What is it, boy?"

"Casement!" I cried. "The Most Noble Thomas Casement, Duke of Hampton!"

"What of him? I know him well."

"*Casement*, my lord!" I repeated. "It is a type of window… It is one which opens[126], such as the larger of the two in Master Tundy's

---

126   Snoop made a sketch of such a window in his entry for Day Eight (page 60).

office. And Master Tundy must know the term, for he must have been responsible for keeping accounts of all your building work. He was trying to tell me it was *Casement* who attacked him. The Duke of Hampton!"

"But I have known his grace for –"

"Grace!" I cried again. "A woman's name!"

His lordship's and my eyes met.

"I'll bet my hat *that's* the name Mary Wood thought she heard one plotter call the other! One of the men you're after is His Grace, the Duke of Hampton!"

"By the Lord Almighty you must be right!" said the Earl of Drayshire. "Anna cannot have taught the imposter girl" – by which he meant Mary – "the correct form of address for each and every noble rank! She took Grace to be a name! Go to the maze, find the girl and ask whether Grace is the name she heard. See if that fills that gap in her recollection! Meanwhile, I will muster my forces. If she answers 'Yes!', then we shall make our next move!"

I sought out Mary Wood and no sooner had I said the word Grace than her eyes widened and her worried face broke into a smile. "Yes!" she said excitedly. "How could I forget? Yes, yes. A thousand times yes!" She paused. "How did you find out?" she asked.

The Earl of Drayshire thought that it was only fit and proper that I should be there for the arrest of the treacherous Thomas Casement, Duke of Hampton. It came as a surprise that Scullion the giant spit-boy was there also; not discovered with the duke but accompanying the earl's party[127]. "I find people are more

---

127   Not a party with cake and balloons but party as in a group of men.

willing to co-operate when Scullion is present," the earl smiled. His Lordship is a man of many surprises.

The end for the traitors came quickly. We burst into the duke's guest chamber – one of the very finest in Goldenhilt Hall, befitting of his rank – and found him seated at a portable writing desk.

"What is the meaning of this?" he demanded. This was quickly followed by cries of, "How dare you?", "Take your hands off me!", some swearing I am reluctant to include here – code or no code – and a final cry of, "The king shall hear of this!"

"And this," said the earl, holding up some documents just found by one of his men searching the room. His eyes read down the page.

The Duke of Hampton fell silent.

"A letter to the King of Spain himself, with talk of a sympathetic ear and plans afoot."

The duke was

being held by Scullion from behind, beside his impressive bed. He had given up struggling. It would have been daffysh[128] to have continued when in the grip of a man too big for

WORDS.

Out of the corner of my eye, I noticed the duke try – with as much subtlety possible – to push something under the bed and out of sight with the tip of his shoe. Something red.

His face dropped when I walked over to him,
bent down and pulled out the item from its
hiding place.

It was a set of plans. A set of plans for the construction of the staircase, including the secret 'priest hole' room. The red was Master Tundy's blood. I felt the anger rise inside me. The steward must either have interrupted their searching his office for it, or been forced to give it to them. Either way, they had stabbed him and he was now at death's door… I raged inside.

"Who is your accomplice, Hampton?" demanded our host.

"How dare you speak to me in that manner!" sneered the duke. "I am your superior![129]"

_____

129   In order of so-called importance, it went dukes, marquises, earls, viscounts, barons. Men either inherited the title on the death of the previous holder of the title, or were given the title by a monarch.

171

"It is Sir Henry Quilt, Father," said The Lady Anna, entering the room, Mary at her side. Everyone's eyes widened at the shock and wonderment of actually seeing the two young women together.

"How do you know with such certainty, daughter?" asked the earl, looking from one child to the other.

"After Thomas here finished asking Mary about Grace, more memories – more images – can back to her," she said. "She left the maze and caught sight of Sir Henry amongst those in the garden. She recognised him at once."

"That I did, my lords," said Mary looking down at her feet. With all pretence of being a lady having gone, she did not hide her awkwardness in such important company.

The Lady Anna squeezed her hand. "Mary came to find me and, when we both returned, he was still there," she said. "He was obviously waiting for someone –" The Lady Anna turned and looked at the duke "– and I knew him to be Sir Henry Quilt."

With the Duke of Hampton still in Scullion's rack-like[130] grip, the earl instructed his men to find Sir Henry Quilt, which they did. He was

---

130   The rack was an instrument of torture, where the victim's arms were tied at one end and their legs at the other, and were stretched.

soon apprehended – putting up the minimum of resistance – and now both he and the duke await the arrival of the king's guards. I suspect that it is only a matter of time until they get a full confession.

This means that my work here at Goldenhilt Hall is done. My work as a *spy,* that is. William de Grieff, the Earl of Drayshire, has asked that I stay on until his guests depart, with his secretary standing in for poor Master Tundy. He feels that I know more than anyone the arrangements that were put into place. I am proud and honoured to continue the work of the loyal and honourable Roger Tundy, for however short a time.

I am also greatly proud of the part I played in thwarting the early stages of a plot to put King Philip of Spain or one of his puppets on the English throne. I only pray that Master Tundy lives, and look I forward to my next mission, wherever it might lead me.

AND
NEXT...?

No records remain of Thomas Snoop's life as a spy, so we can only assume that he was a good one. We do know that he was later knighted for 'services to the crown' and must assume that it was for his undercover work for the shady Lord Severn. John Rider made a full recovery from his mob football injuries and lived to the ripe old age of forty-four. Thankfully, Master Tundy survived the knife attack. It is believed that his rotundity – his roundness – stopped the dagger going in as far as it might have otherwise. Once recovered, he lost a great deal of weight and – though never fit enough to run the Goldenhilt Hall household again – he lived there in comfort in return for his loyal years of service to the de Grieff family. The Lady Anna made a 'good marriage' by marrying into a rich family. Mary Wood made an even better marriage by marrying a man she loved. As for the fight against Catholics? Traitors were usually executed. The first Tudor king, Henry VII, was Catholic, and so was England. Although his son, Henry VIII, broke away from the Church of Rome, England didn't become a protestant country until the reign of his son Edward VI, when the events in this diary took place. When Edward VI died and his half-sister, Mary, became queen, England went back to being a Catholic country again. And she persecuted Protestants. But when *her* half-sister, Elizabeth I, became queen, the country became Protestant again! Elizabeth was the last of the Tudors. She had the first true spymaster, a man named Sir Francis Walsingham.

RAISE YOUR HATS!

It would be surprising if you didn't notice that just about EVERYONE in the excellent illustrations, by Jamie Littler, is wearing a hat most of the time. The bigger the hat, the more important the wearer. As you'll see, most of the labourers are wearing flat caps: low hats for the lower classes. William de Grieff, the Earl of Drayshire, and the Most Noble Thomas Casement, Duke of Hampton, however, have far more impressive affairs, the duke's with a richly decorated band, and held in place with a jewelled broach. The married ladies are mainly wearing the French hood (the peak-shaped head gear). You'll notice that young children and poorer women are wearing the simple coif – often known as 'the biggin' – which was plain white linen and tied under the chin.

A NOTE FROM THE AUTHOR

ONLY THE FACTS ARE TRUE

Although none of the characters in this book are real and there is and was no Goldenhilt Hall, what IS true is the information about such Tudor houses, and life in Tudor times, from sharing beds to mob football. And the Tudor kings and queens, of course.

Another great way to bring history to life is to visit a National Trust property. This will give you a glimpse into the lives of people in the past.

Philip Ardagh